THE RED PILL

TIRTH RAJ PARSANA

THE RED PILL

**_Script & Screenplay
By ~ Aditya Joshi
Featuring : Tirth Parsana_**

Foreword
Preface
Acknowledgements
Prologue

1.
TIRTH'S ROOM - NIGHT 3 AM In Hell Starts
Playing.
DISCLAIMER :
LIBRARY - LATE EVENING 30 Years
Later, YEAR 2054
Part 3
Part 4
LOCAL TRAIN STATION, BUSES,
TREES
Part 6
TIRTH'S LIVING ROOM - DAY/NIGHT
Part 8
LIBRARY - LATE EVENING
PODCAST STUDIO - EVENING
Part 11
Part 12
LIBRARY CAFE - LATE EVENING
Part 14
FOOTPATH - LATE EVENING
TIRTH'S PLACE - NIGHT
LIBRARY - LATE EVENING
ENTITY SUMMON MONTAGE -
DAY/NIGHT
RYAN'S PLACE - NIGHT
TIRTH'S PLACE - NIGHT
Part 21
Part 22
Part 23

TIRTH'S PLACE RESEARCH MONTAGE
- DAY & NIGHT
TIRTH'S ROOM - NIGHT
CAFE - EVENING I Am In A Podcast.

2.
<u>TIRTH'S ROOM - NIGHT</u>
CHURCH - EVENING
Part 28
TIRTH'S PLACE - NIGHT
POV FRIDGE - I GRAB THE GLASS
CEMETRY - NIGHT
Part 32
LIBRARY - LATE EVENING
CAFE - EVENING

3.
<u>RYAN'S PLACE - LATE LATE EVENING</u>
Part 35
MONTAGE SEQUENCE - DAY/NIGHT
Part 37
RYAN'S PLACE - LATE LATE EVENING
STREET - NIGHT
TIRTH'S PLACE - NIGHT
Part 41
CHURCH - NIGHT
TIRTH'S ROOM - NIGHT
LIBRARY - LATE EVENING
TIRTH'S ROOM - NIGHT
LIBRARY - LATE EVENING
TIRTH'S ROOM - NIGHT
Part 48

Your Brain is The Garden of Eden
The Pineal Gland is The Thorne of God & The
Gateway To Heaven
Salvation is SALT The Brain Produces A Salt Fluid
Which Goes Down The Spine
You Must Resurrect This Fluid Through Your
Erectional Energy Back To Your Brain
After Raising Your Salt, You Will Have The "KEY"
into The Kingdom of Heaven
די עליטעס ינוועגטיד רעליגיעז קאו_אפערייששאנז צו מאכן איר
קוקן_ארויס זיד֜ פאר מאכט און מאכן איר זייער שקלאף

Foreword

Tirth Parsana ~ The Biggest Mistake of Nature

Preface

(You're NOW One Step Closer To Reality)

Acknowledgements

Thank You For Enlightening Humanity.

Prologue

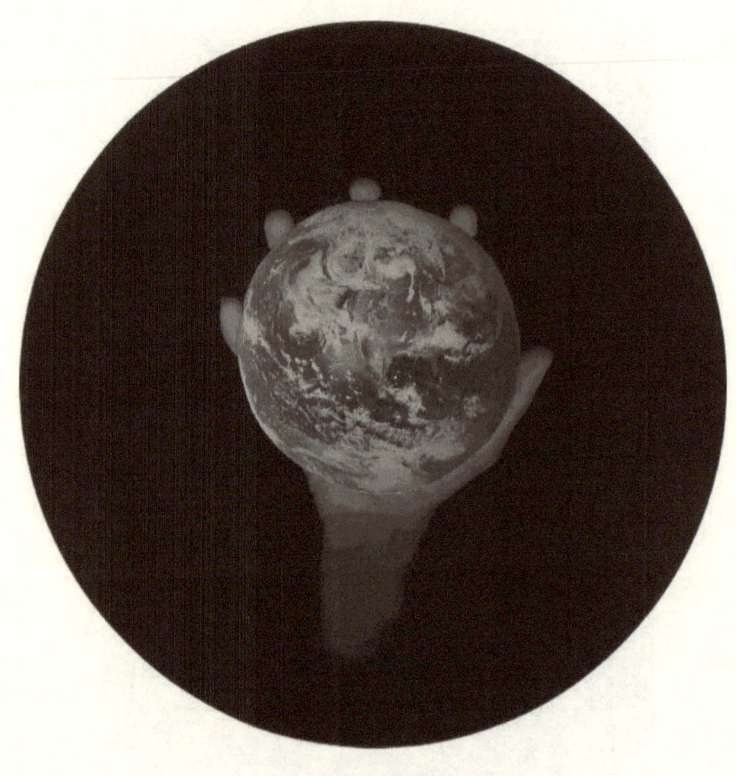

YOU ARE NOW ONE STEP CLOSER
TO REALITY...

CHAPTER ONE

TIRTH'S ROOM - NIGHT 3 AM in Hell starts playing.

A Bluetooth speaker is playing the song.

A montage starts playing which shows the last few months in short snippets and sequential order, somewhat in sync with the lyrics, Actions like writing songs, sitting silently in happy places, recording songs, chilling with friends, at the library, in temples, churches, mosques will all be shown in the montage as hyper lapse of the last few months of my life, the last shot of the montage will be Lucifer back shot, card shot and shot of white light and wind on my face, revealing itself.

(Tirth Parsana; age 21)

come back from the flashback and pause the music on the Bluetooth speaker. I grab my phone, tripod, stabilizer, assemble it all together and set up the frame. I hit record and sit in front of the camera anxiously, and slowly start speaking.

DISCLAIMER :

Watching this video is strictly prohibited for people who are not ready to come out of the illusion that they are living in, I suggest you leave now and keep living that worthless life of yours, and for people who are ready to free their minds... What if I told you everything taught to us about the universe, everything we know about the past right from the times of Gods, every damn thing that mankind has consumed over the years is nothing more than a bunch of well crafted lies, my name is Tirth Parsana I skip intros and come to the straight fucking point, by the time you watch this video I'll be gone already so you either break the shackles of illusion and continue watching this video or leave now and keep mindlessly scrolling and consuming meaningless content.

5, 4, 3, 2, 1 2.

If you're still here, you're now one step closer to reality.

LIBRARY - LATE EVENING 30 Years Later, YEAR 2054

30 Years Later,

YEAR 2054 CUT TO

A few 50-year-olds giving documentary interviews about a common friend, ME. The name of the documentary is "Tirth Parsana: An Unfinished Story." The clapper is kept in front of the interviewer's face.

DOCUMENTARY DIRECTOR (v.o)

Roll Camera, Roll Sound, Claps the clapboard.

DOCUMENTARY DIRECTOR (v.o)

Action !

INTERVIEWER

Good evening sir, for starters, tell us a little about Tirth Parsana and your relation with him

FAIZAL KHAN (age 50)

Tirth Tirth Tirth...

(chuckles)

He helped me a lot in life man, especially when I started making videos and also when I started comedy on stage, he was like a brother to me.

INTERVIEWER

how was Tirth Parsana back then ?

MANAV BHATIA (age 51)

Tirth was always different from others, and today we are all thankful to him for what he has given us. I just hope that he is at peace wherever he is.

Smarni Randive, (age 50)

sits in front of the interviewer.

INTERVIEWER

What were you doing when Tirth went missing ?

SMARNI RANDIVE

I was sticking and circulating missing flyers

INTERVIEWER (v.o) i'm sorry, missing flyers ?

SMARNI RANDIVEyes, missing flyers, matter of fact I still have one with me Smarni pulls out the missing poster from her bag.

LOCAL TRAIN STATION, BUSES, TREES

SMARNI RANDIVE (v.o)

on train stations, buses, random trees everywhere.

Match cut from train stations to buses to trees.

MATCH CUT TO Pull back from the tree and pan to Smarni, age 20 and Manav, age 21. Both Manav and Smarni have hands full of missing flyers

SMARNI RANDIVE (concerned)

bro Manav saat(7) din ho gaye, and we have zero clue Tirth kaha hai

MANAV BHATIA (holds Smarni by her shoulders)

listen Smarni, fat meri bhi rahi hai, but we have to be patient, look at Sahil & Faizal look at how calm they are.

Pan to Sahil & Faizal, both age 20. Faizal (on call, tone is the opposite of calm) hello, ek pura insaan nahi mil raha idhar aur sab baithe hai per pe per chadha ke, kya mazak hai kya Manav & Smarni reaction.

SAHIL PATEL (irritated)

kya javab du uski mummy ko yaar, call pe call aa
raha hai

(shifts to Tirth's mom on call) hello aunty... aunty
tamara kannuda ne hu layi aavis, I will find him and
bring him to you please don't get upset.

SMARNI RANDIVE (sarcastically)

so calm na Soundless visual slow motion close ups
of my friends with a beep and infrared sounds, with
my voiceover.

TIRTH (v.o)

of course you're wondering how this happened. It
all started three months back but before that

who was I, Tirth Parsana.

TIRTH'S LIVING ROOM - DAY/NIGHT

A montage of who I am and my life in Mumbai shown through a single take.

Starts with the shot of "who is Tirth Parsana" searched on a search engine in my laptop, my Instagram comes on top results, click it

TIRTH (v.o; 1) A content creator with 860k followers on Instagram 2. Slow pan to me making a video, 3.Back to the laptop on my YouTube channel.

TIRTH (v.o; 3) and yeah 4M subscribers on YouTube too... 4. Slow 360 pan to my golden play button, to me grabbing it and using it as a dish for eating burger and fries, to posters of "Break The Internet" & Diamond Play Button.

TIRTH (v.o; 4) now most people think I'm lucky that my videos blew up, but only a few know the grind, the hard work, the effort that I put behind this 5. Back to laptop, a web page of my introduction from the site shark times/wikilifeteller,

TIRTH (v.o; 5) You see I was just another boy from GJ 03 6. Back to me, recording a podcast in a podcast setup.

TIRTH (v.o; 6) It took me 7 long years to reach a level where people would actually care to listen about what I had to say 7. Back to laptop, the web page of the site "theparadoxnews.com" on me

TIRTH (v.o; 7) I almost quit after I lost my account three times across different social media platforms, all 100Ks 8. Back to me, dancing in a house party with friends, girls Created using Celtx around me, 6.

TIRTH (v.o; 8) with fame comes wildness that you never knew was within you 9. Back to laptop, Spotify account of me, with 66k monthly listeners,

TIRTH (v.o; 9&10) but this fame made me feel numb, empty on the inside... to overcome the emptiness I let my inner voice out, and that is how I started making music 10. Back to me recording songs. Parsana 11. Back to laptop, "radioandnews.com" website's page titled " INTRODUCING SOCIAL MEDIA'S NEW CHANGE MAKER OF 2023 – Tirth " on me, also a small article showing my estimated net worth to be around 90 lakh Rupees at the age of 20.

TIRTH (v.o; 11) I had everything that I wanted as a kid... money, fame, power, friends, girls, lifestyle you name it. . 12. Back to me, sitting alone in a chaotic setting (feeling lost in and out).

TIRTH (v.o; 12) But there still was emptiness inside me, I felt a feeling that the purpose of my life was different from all of this shit.

LIBRARY - LATE EVENING

ADITYA JOSHI (age 50)

There is something strangely beautiful about people who very randomly get detached from happier places...

JUMP CUT TO

to sad places their minds put them into, Tirth had almost everything at 21 years old, fame, money, power, friends, girls, recognition, but there still was chaos in his head.

INTERVIEWER

what type of chaos ?

MANAV BHATIA

the chaos of unanswered questions. He never really understood the concept of God, he always rebelled against his mom when she gave the credit of his hard work to God, something about religions and God never sat right with him,

and he was always vocal about it

PODCAST STUDIO - EVENING

I am at a studio, giving a podcast.

TIRTH

H2O is a discovery, it existed before we existed, planes, wireless fidelity, television, mobile phones, stuff like that did not exist, we humans created them... therefore these are referred to as...

PODCAST INTERVIEWER

Inventions

TIRTH

Inventions, similarly, I believe that "RELIGION" is a human invention, we created it, but it has drifted away from the very purpose that it was created for.

CUT TO

INTERVIEWER (impressed) wow... With that answer, we come to the end of today's podcast, thank you for your time Tirth

TIRTH

thanks for having me, cheers!

(V.O) cut!

I check my phone, meanwhile the podcast
interviewer comes to me with a hamper,

PODCAST INTERVIEWER

Tirth, a small token of love from our side

TIRTH (decline politely)

no need of this bro

PODCAST INTERVIEWER

please, I insist

TIRTH

aree yaar buddy, your love is enough...bas
(I get a call)

excuse me (receive it and put it on speaker)

TIRTH

hey sugar, what's up!

DATE (v.o)

ullu ke pathe... I've been waiting for almost an hour,
show up in the next ten minutes or this date is over
the girl hangs up the call. I put the phone down, take
a deep breath and look at the podcast interviewer,

The interviewer looks at me, awkward silence.

PODCAST INTERVIEWER

you need the hamper now, don't you

TIRTH

hell yeah !

PODCAST INTERVIEWER

well change of mind

TIRTH

right, change of mind

PODCAST INTERVIEWER

yeah...you're screwed Podcast interviewer re-offers
me the hamper, I take it.

TIRTH

totally Dap, I take the hamper, bro hug. run!

LIBRARY CAFE - LATE EVENING

I enter the library cafe and see the girl paying the bill, I rush towards her breathing heavily,

DATE

don't even try, I'm leaving.

Me heavily breathing switches to normal

TIRTH

okay....

DATE

oh my god, you're not even trying

TIRTH

well, you've already made up your mind, plus I had a really bad fake story to cover up the fact that I totally forgot.

This pisses the girl even more, she slams the book in her hand on the table and leaves. I stand there impervious to the girl leaving.

TIRTH

fair enough I stroll around the cafe, seeing different books, a couple kids recognize me, click pictures. I turn to my table to notice the book,

TIRTH (to the waiter)

bhai, a bottle of mineral water aur ek margherita pizza

The waiter goes to fetch water, Meanwhile I go to the table to read the book's name, As soon as I read the name, my expression changes from calm to bewildered. when the waiter comes back with the bottle, I am gone with the hamper and the book, The waiter finds Rs 1020 cash kept on the table,

(CAMERA TILTS TO)

A silver plate reading

"The books in the library are not for sale"

FOOTPATH - LATE EVENING

Pull out from half revealed book to me walking
hastily with the hamper in my hand,

Chaotic and noisy background filled with many
people.

A couple of guys crash into me, asking for photos,

I get annoyed

TIRTH'S PLACE - NIGHT

I open the hamper, remove a couple of things and then grab the book, remove the book from the hamper - POV HAMPER

The book reveals titled

"How To Summon An Entity"

I start reading, slowly become absorbed, oblivious to the passage of time.

LIBRARY - LATE EVENING

FAIZAL KHAN

After his date, Tirth distanced himself and went into isolation, he wouldn't reply to our calls or messages

SMARNI RANDIVE

He literally started ghosting us and that bugged me a bit, but I let it slide thinking that he was focusing on music.

INTERVIEWER

And what exactly was Tirth doing at this point of time?

MANAV BHATIA (smiles softly)

He found some bizarre book and was literally obsessed with it, he was trying to summon entities.

TIRTH (v.o)

That is correct... after finding the book, in the next few days I kept on trying different ways to summon entities,

But did not even come close to summoning the
slighest of an entity

Now Failure Makes people quit but this failure kept
me trying more and more....

ENTITY SUMMON MONTAGE - DAY/NIGHT

Me reading the last few pages of the book, get up and leave, and before I even realized, only one last way was left to practice... this was comparatively simpler but still more complex than the previous ones Firstly, no sunlight for 6 days, I used black papers and cloth to block sunlight from entering Me sticking black chart papers and cloth on every window of the house, even bathroom windows On the 6th night,

I drew a pentacle and placed a candle on each of the five elements spirit, air, water, earth and fire, Multiple shots of me drawing a pentacle, placing candles on each five elements the only step left was to manifest it all happening, which was easier said than done, the candle would blow out by itself on the smallest shift of focus I close eyes to manifest and get a little disturbed, the candle blows out, after three failed attempts, I was extremely frustrated but still decided to give it one last shot

I close eyes and start focusing, the flame slowly starts getting disturbed, more disturbed, blows out, I open my eyes and see the candle blown.

TIRTH

areee yaaaarrrrr...

I lose temper, grab the book, tear it violently and throw it, the friction causes a small cut in my hand, a drop of blood falls on the candle and the frame re-ignites, I notice the flame, then notice a half-faced CD in the book's torn front cover, I remove it, insert it in my laptop and watch the video Video of Ryan explaining the process starts playing in laptop

RYAN'S PLACE - NIGHT

RYAN

how many times did you fail huh? (laughs)

I failed 12 times and, in the 13th try understood what
I or rather we have been doing wrong, just like you
found the CD in the front cover

(v.o) you will find a card in the back cover, about
the card, try not being too judgmental and place it in
the center of your pentacle and then

Montage of me tearing the back cover, finding the
card, matching with Ryan's v.o in background

then with the power of your thoughts and
channelization of your energy into the card,
manifest... manifest with all your might, manifest
maniacally, go berserk, because he who you
summon is neither darkness nor light but one of the
greatest forces, a force beyond measure, a force that
no archangel and no demon messes with

I get shocked, mannequin

TIRTH'S PLACE - NIGHT

I place the card in the center of the pentacle,

I close my eyes to focus, the candle's flame burns brightly,

ENTRY BGM STARTS PLAYING, EXTREME WIDE DRONE SHOT POV LUCIFER: CLOSING IN ON A BUILDING

I remain focused, The POV is now closer to the building,

The card of the devil in the pentagon, flame burning POV super close, enters the house through the open gallery, into the living room, stops behind me,

I slowly open my eyes, a pair of legs are behind me, I turn to see a young, attractive man in an all-black attire, wearing a long trench coat standing behind me, he comes around and stands in front of me, I pick the card up, get up slowly and stand face to face

TIRTH

please have a seat...

(Both of us sit.)

are you the devil?

LUCIFER

I am Lucifer, tell me what is the causeth of thee
summoning me

TIRTH

Ever since I was a child, I felt a feeling that
everything we humans know about this universe is a

LUCIFER

Lie

Lucifer starts laughing hysterically for 10 to 15
seconds,

TIRTH

right

LUCIFER

what does thee wanteth from me

TIRTH

come on...you knew what I felt, you know what I
want

LUCIFER

No, I can't tell them to you... you're not worthy

TIRTH

I'm not worthy without giving me a chance?

LUCIFER

fair enough

(throws the coin at tirth) flip the coin once on both
the sides... once and you're eligible

I flip the coin and it comes on heads,

Lucifer who was sitting opposite to me suddenly
appears beside me, and whispers in my ears

LUCIFER

(whispers)

you'll keep getting heads,

all you have to do is get tails once. You have 24
hours, to get tails, just flip the coin.

(Lucifer disappears)

I start flipping the coin and keeps getting heads,
Night turns into day and I am still trying,

A montage shows me flipping coins at different
places like bathroom, bedroom, living room, kitchen
etc, and getting pissed as the coin keeps flipping on
heads in every single try.

The 24-hour time period is almost over, one last
minute is left, I quit and keep the coin aside

TIRTH

It won't happen, it just won't happen Lucifer
reappears,

LUCIFER

Let me repeat what I said 24 hours back, you're not
worthy

I hear the clock ticking, clock ticking also in frame
Something suddenly strikes me,

I run back into my mind and replay what Lucifer
told me.

LUCIFER

(flashback)

You'll keep getting heads (v.o)

all you have to do is get tails once, my eyes widen

you have 24 hours I grab and flip the coin,

LUCIFER

(v.o)

to get tails I catch the coin

LUCIFER

(v.o)

just flip the coin I flip the coin.

It is tails, I smile and then start laughing.

LUCIFER

you have successfully passed the eligibility test.

TIRTH

before you unfold these secrets, I want to know the
point of this test.

LUCIFER

(smirks)

every neuro cell in our mind has its own small brain, we know the existence of many languages, but we learn only a couple of them, so the neuro cells in our mind related to other languages remain unused and you know what slowly happens to them

TIRTH

(realizes)

they stop functioning

LUCIFER

(nods in agreement with a wicked smile on face)

For years Tirth, you and every other person in this world have only been shown one side of the coin,

so often that you'll are now used to it,

this story is not meant for those who stay on the course of fate, only those who cheat and flip the course of destiny deserve this story of people who changed fate forever.

TIRTH

(exhales)

I have been waiting for this moment for the longest
time,

I am ready, tell me

LUCIFER

tell you...so easy so simple right but (sings)where is
the fun in that

Devil starts laughing and stops abruptly

LUCIFER CHAPTER NUMBER 1

Adam's Personal Diary, a book said to be written by
Adam's point of view, so blasphemous that it was
declared

heresy by the Church and banned from the Bible...
YEAH... and another book, a gospel that explains
the true God and the evil

TIRTH

what about these books

LUCIFER

what about these books? Adam, Eve, the serpent,
their sons, the God, Devil and Gnosticism

TIRTH

um, what are you talking about Lucifer looks
towards the side, a vase falls,

I turn to look at the vase, when I turn back to look at
Lucifer, he is right beside my ear, he snaps.

I get caught off guard.

LUCIFER

(mumbles fumingly)

if you cannot break down what I am talking about
you don't deserve to know the truth

(deep manly voice)

break down the secrets for yourself, I won't serve
them in a golden platter to you.

Lucifer disappears.

TIRTH'S PLACE
RESEARCH MONTAGE
- DAY & NIGHT

A montage of me starting the search starts,

I stand up, take a pen and paper and write down the
names that Lucifer mentioned.

I start searching on the search engine,

I search for the book on the search engine and get to
know the book's name is The Apocalypse of Adam.

A softboard starts filling up with images and texts
that I keep finding,

I find theories on different websites and get to
access the

books both Apocalypse of Adam & Secret Gospel of
John

I read more and more about their readings and keep
making notes on the softboard.

I divide the content based on the hints and start
filling these hints.

The connections between the images and texts start
to increase more and more.

1.   INT. TIRTH'S PLACE - NIGHT

At the end of the montage, I write the last words
Gnostics were all about understanding self-
knowledge on a paper and stick it on the softboard
and make its connection to Gnosticism,

TIRTH

I think I broke down all the hints.

LUCIFER

I've been waiting to hear this.

Tirth gets startled but starts explaining everything
ANIMATION & SHOOT BOTH.

CHAPTER NUMBER 1 - THE APOCALYPSE OF
ADAM & SECRET GOSPEL OF JOHN

TIRTH

(v.o)

The secret banned book written by Adam's is called
The Apocalypse of Adam as he tells his son about
the creation of humanity and the coming flood.

Adam and Eve, they rebelled against God, but not
the true God,

A false Evil Creator God who is the ruler of the
materialistic world. The Apocalypse of Adam is the
banned book from the point of view of the rebels
that the Church doesn't want us to know.

LUCIFER

Why does the church not want you'll to know?

TIRTH

Because Adam reveals... that the Evil Creator God is
actually the Devil and created humanity to be his
slaves. But there's a hidden way for humanity to
escape.

Lucifer starts laughing hysterically.

TIRTH

According to the Apocalypse of Adam, he and Eve
were divine powerful beings, more powerful than
the God we worship, Adam quotes.

Lucifer cuts him and says the quote.

LUCIFER

he quotes "and we resembled the great eternal angels, for we were higher than the God who had created us and the powers with him." To understand this, you have to know that the Church banned many books. And these banned books partially form what's known as Gnosticism.

TIRTH

And those who followed these secret teachings were a group of heretical Christian rebels known as Gnostics. Gnostic comes from the Greek word for knowledge.

So, Gnostics are those who claim to know the secret knowledge.

Another banned Gnostic book you mentioned is the Apocryphon of John.

In this secret book, it is revealed that the God of the Bible is an evil, Satanic being, a false God. The true God is an eternal divine mind, pure thought. And this divine mind begins to structure itself. And it expressed itself through a divine human.

This means that humanity is divine, an expression, a form of the true God, a being of pure thought.

It suggests that humanity is actually higher than the God of the Bible, which is a fractured, malformed being. The God of the Bible, who is the Lord of the

material world rather than divine mind, became
enraged at the fact that humanity was higher than
him and trapped the perfect divine human into the
prison of a material body and threw it into the
material world to limit its power and to make it into
its slave.

LUCIFER

In addition to trapping the divine human in a
material body and the world of matter, to further
limit its power, he split the human in two into Adam
and Eve. Adam said, "Then God, the ruler of the
Eons and the powers divided us in wrath, and we
served him in fear and slavery."

TIRTH

So, he basically entombed them in a body,
imprisoned them in the garden, wiped their memory
and split them in two to keep them from realizing
their power and divinity.

LUCIFER

that is correct, tell me what you found about the two
trees in the Garden of Eden

ANIMAMATION & SHOOT BOTH.

TIRTH

The two trees in the Garden of Eden are two very important trees, the Tree of Life and the Forbidden Tree from which Adam & Eve were not allowed to have food, the Tree of Knowledge.

According to Gnostics, the Tree of Life is there to further trap humanity by making them more primal and animalistic. The Tree of Life injects them with the artificial spirit or false life.

Here's a brilliant poetic description, which I love, of the so-called Tree of Life from the secret Gospel of John.

LUCIFER

"Its root is bitter, its branches are dead. Its shadow is hatred. Its leaves are deception. The nectar of wickedness is in its blossoms. Its fruit is death. Its seed is desire.

Its flowers are in darkness. Those who eat from it are denizens of Hades.

Darkness is their resting place." ANIMATION & SHOOT BOTH.

TIRTH

(impressed reaction; v.o)

Tree of Knowledge, the Forbidden tree ironically represents higher thinking, purposeful thought, intuition, insight and conceptualization. It's what the Gnostics called epinaoi and is directly related to the Neocortex. So, where the Tree of Life is associated with animalistic, primal, instinctual urges, The forbidden Tree of Knowledge is associated with the mind and thought. These trees couldn't be more different.

What the Evil Creator God is trying to do is make humanity more animalistic and deny us the capacity of thought and attaining knowledge, because he wants us to be his slaves. And he knows that if we acquire knowledge and purposeful thinking, we will be able to become self-aware of our own divinity and become more powerful than him.

The Bible explicitly mentions three sons Cain, Abel and Seth. According to the Gnostics, Cain and Abel's father wasn't Adam. Instead, Cain and Abel were born from the rape of Eve by the evil creator God. So it was Seth that was the true son of Adam and Eve.

Remember that Adam and Eve were originally one divine being that was

split. So Seth, being the offspring of Adam and Eve, symbolically represent the reunion of the divine.

In other words, Seth had the united power of divinity hidden within him. And this idea was so important to the Gnostics that those who believed this were called Sethians. The reason it's so important to the Sethian Gnostics is because everyone else is killed in the flood, except for the line of Seth and Noah, which went on to populate the entire human race.

LUCIFER

Symbolically, this means that every single human has the hidden power of divinity within them, that they can become all powerful and escape the material world,

In the Brihadaranyaka Upanishad of Hinduism, lies a quote "Brahma satyam jagan mithyā"- Brahman is real; the world is illusory

I get shocked to see Lucifer quote.

LUCIFER

you look for clues and you find them everywhere, anyways, in the story, Adam goes on to warn Seth about the coming flood that will occur.

TIRTH

that is correct, yes

Now, in the Bible, God sends a flood to drown everyone except for Noah and his family, because the rest of the world is sinful, while Noah is righteous and obedient. However, Adam tells his son that this is wrong.

The real reason God sends a flood is because he's angry that those from the line of Seth refuse to be his slaves and are rebelling.

This is because they contain that seed

of divinity within, passed down from Adam and Eve through Seth. But God sees that Noah and his family will still serve him.

So what God does is he sends down a flood to destroy and drown the entire world except for Noah and his family and the animals on the ark.

But unbeknownst to this evil creator god, divine beings from the higher realms of mind save the descendants of Seth by hiding them in a cloud of light.

So God sends a flood, drowns the world.

And after this, after the flood is over, god strikes a deal with Noah. God tells Noah that if he agrees to be his slave and to populate the world with those that will be his slaves, he will give the earth to Noah

and his descendants and make them great kings and
rulers.

LUCIFER

God says to Noah, "behold, I have protected you in
the ark along with your wife and your sons and their
wives and their animals and the birds of heaven.
Therefore, I will give the Earth to you, you and your
sons, in kingly fashion. You will rule over it, you
and your sons. And no seed will come from you of
the men who will not stand in my presence in
another glory." Noah agrees to this and tells his sons
about this deal he struck with the evil God.

TIRTH

Then Noah divides the whole earth among his sons.
He says to them

"My sons, listen to my words. Behold, I have
divided the Earth among you, but serve him in fear
and serve him in slavery all the days of your life.
Let

not your seed depart from the face of God the
Almighty."

But then the descendants of Seth are returned to
Earth from the cloud of light. And when the God of
the material world discovers that there are people
who aren't worshipping him and refuse to be his

slaves, he gets furious, thinking that Noah betrayed him. So God confronts Noah, but Noah confirms these are not his generations, he says "I shall testify in front of your might, these people have not originated from me or my sons."

According to the Apocalypse of Adam, the Earth is now populated by the Sethians that refuse to worship the Evil creator God and are striving to unlock the divine within themselves. But it's also populated by those that have made a deal with this God and have chosen the opposite path and have become slaves to this so called God.

According to the Gnostics, this represents the situation that we are in right now, and it's symbolic for Gnostic Christianity versus what would eventually become mainstream Christianity.

TIRTH

Gnostics believed in reincarnation and the continuous imprisonment of the soul in matter. So for the Gnostics, the only way to escape the material world is to achieve Gnosis, that is, knowledge about what you truly are and ascend to divinity.

Where mainstream Christianity is about faith, sin, repentance and worshipping God, Gnosticism is about knowledge, seeing through the illusion of the

material world and becoming God. The Gnostics
were all about understanding secret knowledge.

LUCIFER

So what do you think Tirth?

What makes more sense, even just as a story? Do
you think the God of the Bible seems like a good
loving God or an evil Satanic being? Do you think
that faith, worship, sin and repentance make more
sense or self knowledge, understanding and
unlocking inner divinity?

I'm about to give him an answer

LUCIFER

uh uh uh uh uh... rhetorical questions

that was just chapter 1 out of three, before we go
further, try living that materialistic life of yours for
some time again, and try living it peacefully.

TIRTH

why do you say that

LUCIFER

Because I can see the near future,

your life is at risk in the near future, bad things will
happen to you.

Lucifer disappears.

I sit there alone cluelessly.

TIRTH'S ROOM - NIGHT

I am speaking in front of the phone.

TIRTH

the next few days were really messed up, to know
the secrets was tough but it was tougher to hold on
to these secrets.

1.   EXT. CAFE - EVENING I am in a podcast.

TIRTH

we humans have been lied to since the dawn of time,
we do not belong here we are trapped in this cycle
of endless materialism and everything you have
been taught is wrong, we are doing false activities in
the names of rituals to please the Almighty, it is the
wrong G..

Tirth exhales

PODCAST INTERVIEWER 2

okay bro par mai toh sirf yeh pucha tha ki what do
you feel about the rising prices in petrol and diesel?

I make an irritated face.

TIRTH

thankyou for inviting me, cut all of this and have a
good day

I get up and leave.

TIRTH

(v.o)

all the places that I once had fun at

Flashback of me and my friends at a turf playing
football, beach, party at home

now meant nothing to me. In the next few days, all I
could think about was Chapter 1 and what would be
Chapter 2 and 3,

To me zoned out at the same places while friends
are enjoying

CAFE - EVENING I am
in a podcast

TIRTH

we humans have been lied to since the dawn of time,
we do not belong here we are trapped in this cycle
of endless materialism and everything you have
been taught is wrong, we are doing false activities in
the names of rituals to please the Almighty, it is the
wrong G..

(Tirth exhales)

PODCAST INTERVIEWER 2

okay bro par mai toh sirf yeh pucha tha ki what do
you feel about the rising prices in petrol and diesel?

I make an irritated face.

TIRTH

thankyou for inviting me, cut all of this and have a
good day

I get up and leave.

TIRTH

(v.o)

all the places that I once had fun at

Flashback of me and my friends at a turf playing
football, beach, party at home

now meant nothing to me. In the next few days, all I
could think about was Chapter 1 and what would be
Chapter 2 and 3,

To me zoned out at the same places while friends
are enjoying

TIRTH'S ROOM - NIGHT

TIRTH
(me speaking in front of the tripod setup)
never before had I wanted to shout at the top of
my voice so badly, so loud that the entire world
would listen to what I wanted to say.
But I did not, I curbed the voice inside me for so
long that I could not
hold it in any longer, and that... is when I did
something stupid.

CHURCH - EVENING

The Sunday evening prayer is going on, everyone is sitting and praying and among them am I too,

But I sit very atheistically while others are wholly involved.

The prayer ends, everyone gets up, some start talking with each other and others proceed to leave.

I get up, go towards the center and start speaking loudly

TIRTH ATTENTION PEOPLE!

The father, age 50 years old, turns back to look at Tirth, People start closing in on Tirth.

TIRTH

We humans have been praying to the wrong God, we have the divinity hidden within ourselves, we Ourselves are Gods !

RANDOM MAN

Who the hell are you kid ?

TIRTH

I am the biggest mistake of nature, but you can
consider me a messenger

RANDOM MAN

I don't think you get what I'm saying, who the hell
are you to tell us if we are worshipping the wrong
God or the right God

TIRTH

you have to take my word on it sir,

RANDOM LADY

We don't need a word from an atheist like you,

(Some men close in on me)

TIRTH

why do y'all not understand

RANDOM MAN

(close to me, speaks a little softly)

hey kid, stop making a fool out of yourself and leave
now

TIRTH

I am not the fool in this conversation sir, you'll are!
Believe me...

The man swings at me and I get caught off guard,
four to five men start attacking me

RANDOM MAN

We don't need retards like you to teach us about our
God and religion... is that clear?

My mouth starts bleeding, I start laughing,

They beat me up more, MID CU OF FATHER

The father intervenes.

FATHER

that's it, quit hitting the boy, STOP!

The men stop beating and listen to the father Father
closes in talking to the men,

FATHER

only a fool, asks for a sorry from a fool...

A wise man feels sorry for the fool

The men look down in shame of what they just did.

FATHER

(c'ntd)

I shall personally ask God for forgiveness of this
kid's sins, Go home gentlemen

(bids them goodbye) See you next Sunday

The men leave.

Father gives me a hand to get up. I look at the father
with respect.

TIRTH

(ungratefully)

I don't need you to ask your God for forgiveness on
my behalf.

FATHER

people equipped with half knowledge don't change societies son,

(points at the lifeline on his palm)

they only change these lifelines of their own,

We expected better off you TIRTH

what do you mean we ?

FATHER

go home and find out for yourself

I realize, I rush out of the church, go back to my
place.

TIRTH'S PLACE - NIGHT

TIRTH

Lucifer, I am sorry, I made an impulsive decision, this should not have happened,

hey where are you, Lucifer?

I search the whole house, but don't find him, I sit disappointedly, look down at the floor.

LUCIFER

I already made the prediction young man, you failed to take notes,

look at you, has only heard Chapter 1 and tries to change the society

Lucifer starts laughing hysterically,

Seeing him laugh Tirth chuckles and laughs softly too Lucifer stops laughing abruptly and yells at Tirth.

LUCIFER

(shouts)

STOP LAUGHING YOU IMBECILE!

I stop laughing at once, get shocked,

A vase, a glass and some cutleries fall on the ground, I get startled and look,

Lucifer comes right beside me and holds my chin tight

LUCIFER

(c'ntd)

you have done the dumbest thing that you could have, and it is funny to you, what are we playing huh, (sings) Dumb Ways To Die?

Lucifer pushes Tirth's chin back

TIRTH

This was the first and last mistake, (Lucifer tidies his coat)

This won't happen again Lucifer sits back at his position.

LUCIFER

Whenever the Quran speaks about blessings
received by the Prophets, it specifically mentions
the gift of Intellect.

This is just one of the many verses about it, from
surah Baga rah:

"He gives wisdom unto whom he will, and he unto
whom wisdom is given, he truly hath received
abundant good. But none remember... except men of
understanding."

Do you understand Tirth ?

TIRTH

(softly) yes, I do

LUCIFER

louder

TIRTH

(normal tone) yes, I do

LUCIFER

(shouts) LOUDER!

TIRTH

(shouts loudly) yes I do, YES I DO,

YES LUCIFER, I DO!

LUCIFER

(switches from angry to his normal self)

Alright then, CHAPTER NUMBER TWO - THE
SECRET GOSPEL OF JUDAS

TIRTH

you won't give me hints, just say it directly?

LUCIFER

well, I have been a little harsh on you, so I thought
why not also go a little easy on you or whatever
whatever.

TIRTH

okay, go on then

LUCIFER

no no no I won't tell this to you, someone else will,
someone who knows the story in and out,

but how to reach that someone is for you to figure
out, ahhhhh! I just casually rhymed words, am I the
coolest or what

(laughs)

(pulls out a page/sheet of paper)

(from his coat and keeps it in front of me)

here's your hint, do not take much time or you
might end up in a worse place than today

Lucifer disappears.

I examine the paper closely, The paper is completely
blank.

TIRTH

him and his hints man

I leave the paper in the living room, get up and
leave.

A shot of two halves of a big lemon and an earbud
in Tirth's kitchen.

A FEW HOURS LATER...

I go in the kitchen to grab a glass of flavored
creatine from the refrigerator.

POV FRIDGE - I GRAB THE GLASS

while leaving, for a split second I look at the lemon
and earbuds but leave,

Midway through the passage, I realize something
and rush back into the kitchen.

I look at the half-cut lemon, touch the earbuds, they
are soaked.

I grab a candle and matchbox, rush back towards the
paper kept in the living room,

Grab the paper, light the candle and slide the paper
horizontally a little above the flame.

The hidden numbers slowly reveal in a brownish
shade, I take a good look at them.

These numbers are location coordinates. I search the
coordinates on maps,

The location reveals to be a cemetery.

CEMETRY - NIGHT

I reach the cemetery, and find no one over there, I feel a bit tense,

I find a place to sit, hesitate at first but finally sit. STILL FRAME DISSOLVES TO SHOW TIME PASSING BY

I keep waiting, sitting, start dozing off a bit, sleep asymmetrically in the place I was sitting.

POV SHOT - CLOSING IN ON ME.

I am sleeping, a hand shakes me and calls out my name

FATHER

Tirth...Tirth I don't respond

FATHER

(loudly)

TIRTH

I wake up alarmingly, and see the Father from the church Flashback

FATHER

people equipped with half knowledge don't change societies son,

(points at the lifeline on his palm)

they only change these lifelines of their own,

We expected better off you TIRTH

You are the father from the church, and you are the guy that Lucifer was talking about

FATHER

that is correct son, I unfold the forthcoming chapter

TIRTH

(chuckles) this is crazy

FATHER

well now it starts to get crazier,

CHAPTER NUMBER TWO - THE SECRET GOSPEL OF JUDAS

Judas the betrayer. He's been considered one of the most villainous characters of the Bible. But only a few know that there's a secret Gospel of Judas.

Now, like Judas himself, the Gospel of Judas was despised by the Church.

TIRTH

why?

FATHER

Because... in this heretical Gospel, Jesus Christ himself reveals that everything that we know about mainstream Christianity is wrong.

Jesus takes Judas aside and reveals to him secrets about the creation of the world, that the twelve disciples are evil, and that God is actually the devil.

Now, according to the Gospel of Matthew, Judas betrayed Christ for 30 pieces of silver. However, the Gospel of Judas paints a much more intricate and heretically blasphemous picture.

How this book that was considered lost to time was recovered is a beautiful story in itself, but for some other day

Having survived its 1700-year journey, what do we find within the pages of the betrayer's Gospel?

TIRTH

I don't know,

Is Judas even a betrayer at all?

Father smirks, ANIMATION & SHOOT

FATHER

When Jesus came up to his disciples sitting together
praying over the bread he laughed.

Animation starts

The disciples said to him "master, why are you
laughing at our prayer? What have we done? This is
what's right."

"I'm not laughing at you. You're not doing this
because you want to, but because through this your
God will be praised."

"Master, you are the son of our God." Jesus said to
them "how do you know me? Truly I say to you no
generation of the people among you will ever know
me."

(v.o, disciples getting angry animation)

When his disciples heard this, they started to get
angry and furious and started to curse him in their
hearts.

But when Jesus noticed their ignorance, he said to them "why are you letting your anger trouble you? Has your God within you and his stars become angry with your souls? If any of you is strong enough among humans to bring out the perfect humanity stand up and face me."

(v.o, all disciples looking at each other, judas raises hand and stands up)

None of the disciples had the courage to stand up except for one.

Judas was able to stand up and told Jesus "I know who you are and where you've come from. You've come from the immortal realm of barblo and I'm not worthy to utter the name of the one who sent you." You see, Judas was stronger than the other disciples and unlike the others he knows who Jesus really is and that he doesn't come from the God that the disciples worship.

Seeing that strength and perceptiveness of Judas Jesus said, "Come and I'll teach you about the mysteries that no human will see.

Because there exists a great and boundless realm whose horizons no angelic generation has seen, in which is a great invisible spirit, which no angelic eye has ever seen, no heart has ever comprehended, and it's never been called by any name. And a luminous cloud appeared there, and he the Spirit

said, let an angel come into being to attend me. And
a great angel, the self-begotten, the God of the light,
emerged from the cloud and he said, let a luminous
realm come into being. And it came into being.

And that's how he created the rest of the realms of
light."

Animation stops, Real time

Jesus is revealing to Judas that the true God is a
luminous divine mind and generated a realm of light

Jesus also reveals to Judas that the God that created
Adam and Eve which is the God the disciples
worship and the same God of what would become
mainstream Christianity today isn't the true God at
all. That it's actually an immensely evil being and
one of the rulers of chaos in Hades.

The true God is a divine mind from which all things
emanate. He says, "So I am not the son of the God
described

in the Bible, which is an evil satanic ruler of chaos,
the devil. Rather, I come from the immortal realm of
the divine mind."

Judas recognized this while the other disciples
didn't.

TIRTH

So, Jesus is a messenger from the immortal realm
sent to wake humanity up to the fact that they are
divine and that they don't need to worship the evil
creator God but that they can tap into their own
inner divinity through understanding the secret
knowledge of what they truly are.

FATHER

That's the message according to the Gospel of
Judas. Now, according to some scholars, the Gospel
of Judas is a challenge to the church's authority.
Since many bishops would claim their authority as
church leaders as coming through a direct line to
Jesus's first disciples. The Gospel of Judas attempts
to demolish this by saying the disciples worshipped
a false evil God that they and their generations will
lead astray the faithful engage in murder, human
sacrifice and will never know Christ.

In other words, what would become orthodox
Christianity according to the Gospel of Judas is
actually a false gospel and the opposite of truth. It's
the gospel of the Satanic creator God. But what
about human sacrifice? Well, it's believed by some
that this is a criticism of church leaders that would
encourage martyrdom or dying for Christ during the
persecution of the Romans.

Judas certainly is not a hero in this story, far from it. Nonetheless, he's much closer to the truth than the other disciples. And Jesus reveals the hidden truth to Judas. But the story

takes a crazy and unbelievable twist.

You see, many scholars originally thought that the Gospel of Judas portrayed Judas in a relatively positive light, that he was a hero compared to the other disciples and that Judas was a friend to Jesus, that his betrayal wasn't really a betrayal, that was just him following Jesus's orders.

But all that was about to change, upon a closer look at the Gospel, something far more sinister was revealed. Jesus refers to Judas as the 13th demon when he says to Judas, "why are you all worked up, you 13th demon?" Now, 13 references the fact that once Judas is replaced as a disciple, there will be a total of 13 disciples.

And the Gospel of Judas is a gnostic text. 13 is associated with the demonic creator God, as he is sometimes known as the ruler of the 13 realms.

Animation starts; (Arkansas, Judas and Jesus talking)

Arkansas, are the demons that rule the material world. Judas said, "surely my seed doesn't dominate the rulers, does it?"

"come, let me tell you about the holy generation. Not so that you'll go there, but so you'll be sorry when you see the kingdom and all its generation. You'll become the 13th and will be cursed by other generations and will rule over them, and your star will rule over the 13th realm." "Truly I tell you, Judas, those who offer sacrifices to sackless everything that's evil, but you'll do more than all of them because you'll sacrifice the humanity which bears me. Your horn has already been raised, your anger has been kindled, your star

has ascended, and your heart has strayed. The star that leads the way is your star."

Animation ends, Real time

TIRTH

To me, it is crystal clear that Judas is no benevolent hero in this story. Based on this information, we can come to a few possible conclusions that Judas was secretly the Satanic creator God the whole time, or that his soul will eventually become promoted to the Satanic creator God, the most villainous entity in all reality.

FATHER

So what is the message of the Gospel of Judas?

TIRTH

This gospel is meant to warn the people of the world
that they shouldn't be led astray by the teachings of
the twelve disciples and what has become
mainstream Christianity. Because as long as they
did, they would unconsciously remain servants of
the satanic creator God and never reach the truly
divine, immortal realm. They would never
understand the Sanskrit term from the Mandukya
Upanishad, Ayam ātmā brahma - "This Self, which
is the Atman is God", they would never realize their
own divinity.

Father is impressed by the answer,

FATHER

I can see why he chose you

TIRTH

chose me... who chose me, lucifer?

father smiles and nods slightly

TIRTH

(c'ntd)

huh? I think there's some misunderstanding father,
he has not chosen me, I have summoned him.

FATHER

(chuckles)

that is exactly what I used to think too,

a prediction is a blessing, a prediction is a curse, if
you want to change a man's life, just make a
prediction of what is going to happen to them,

exactly what the witches did in Shakespeare's
Macbeth

exactly what Jesus did with Judas,

and exactly what Lucifer did with you... and I

I get slightly shocked and slightly confused.

TIRTH

what are you trying to say?

FATHER

Just like he predicted that your life was in danger, he
made a prediction about me too,

(1ˢᵗ version, father mimics Lucifer)

he said, " You father, will not be told the last
chapter, but you will save the life of and later
narrate chapter two to the chosen person."

(2ⁿᵈ version, flashback to Lucifer tells father in
church)

LUCIFER

You father, will not be told the last chapter, but it is
you who will save the life of and later narrate
chapter two to the chosen person

Father nods.

(cut back to me)

TIRTH

that is just ridiculous, I'm not buying any of that

FATHER

you believe it or not, this is and shall remain the
truth,

I believe my purpose is now fulfilled, but yours is
not son

TIRTH

what comes next

FATHER

I don't know, but good luck to you for whatever it is

He offers me his hand to shake, we shake hands
Father leaves.

LIBRARY - LATE EVENING

30 years later, documentary sequence

MANAV BHATIA

Tirth had now ghosted us for almost like a month,
we thought he was caught up with something
important, so we did not bother him much, but the
very next thing that happens is a message from Tirth
pops up on our group chat saying, "would anyone of
you by any chance know anything about tarot."

And I happened to know a friend who read tarot.

CAFE - EVENING

I am already sitting in the cafe,

The tarot card reader enters, we greet.

TIRTH

Hi, Tirth Parsana

ELLY

yes, I've seen you on the internet, I am Elly btw

TIRTH

Hi Elly, you read tarot?

ELLY

yes I do

TIRTH

great, what do you think about this card

I pull out the card,

Elly examines the card closely.

ELLY

Well, this very obviously is a tarot card of the devil

But there's something strange about this card like...
like in a way that it gives me mixed energies

TIRTH

(confused tone)

mixed energies like positive and negative?

ELLY

(affirmative tone)

yes...YES like positive and negative but I don't
know much about this

TIRTH

arey yaar

ELLY

I'm sorry I really wish I could help you

TIRTH

please tell me you know a someone who knows
something

ELLY

I'm sorry, I don't.

I get a little upset and stand up to leave.

TIRTH

I'll take your leave, thanks!

ELLY

wait, you can try your luck with my tarot tutor, see
if he knows something or someone

(I sit back at excitedly)

TIRTH

I can shoot my shot for sure, yes

ELLY

okay, here's his card, it has his phone number and
address

see if it is the will of he who remains

TIRTH

he who remains...interesting I take the card and rush
out.

CHAPTER THREE

RYAN'S PLACE - LATE LATE EVENING

I climb the stairs of Ryan's place and ring his bell,
He opens after 3 4 bells. Ryan's face reveals,
I get shocked to see the exact same man that I saw
in the CD found from the book
Flashback of the video playing
RYAN
hi do we know each other
TIRTH
you don't know me, but I know you
you are the guy who was teaching how to
summon an entity
Ryan gets slightly shocked and happy,
RYAN
small world right...come on in my friend
I enter inside his house,
RYAN
hey you don't have to call me the guy from the
video, call me Ryan
TIRTH
nice to meet you Ryan, my name is Tirth
Ryan takes me to the room where he shot the
video, there are a few candles, a deck of tarot cards.
RYAN

please make yourself at home Tirth

TIRTH

sure thanks

I observe the room and get flashbacks of the
video, Ryan gets two glasses of water and sits in front
of me,

He looks at me right in the eye, with passion in
his eyes he speaks

RYAN

(passionately)

I thought I would be the one who knocks but
might that, destiny prevails a someone
higher and knocks me out

Ryan flicks a candle with his finger and starts
laughing, he looks at the candles and starts speaking,
even these candles light up Snaps his fingers,
in the presence of that one, THE CHOSEN ONE !

(points at Tirth)

He saw something in you that I can just wish I
had, and that is my sorrow,

You know I could flip the world upside down,
even if for one night this that you have, I could
borrow.

TIRTH

how can you say it with so much conviction that I
am the chosen one, it could be you too

RYAN

NAH... it is not me, it is you... all that is
happening, all of this... the flow of these events was
precisely spoiler to me by Lucifer.

TIRTH

what do you mean ?!

RYAN

It was tough, after several hundred tries, I finally
summoned Lucifer, there he was sitting

exactly where you are !

NO CUTS IN SHOT JUST PAN TO LUCIFER
SITTING INSTEAD OF TIRTH WITH MILD
LIGHT CHANGE AFTER RYAN'S DIALOGUE

(Flashback)

LUCIFER

You dear Ryan have been chosen for a very special
purpose

Ryan listens curiously

LUCIFER

(c'ntd)

you will make a video explaining this ritual that you
did to summon me,

MONTAGE SEQUENCE - DAY/NIGHT

Montage of Lucifer's (v.o) with Ryan performing

Go in as much detail as you can Ryan speaking in the video

you will then put this video in a CD Ryan putting the video in a CD,

put the CD in the front cover of the book that I give you,

Book being given, Ryan putting the CD in the book's front cover,

a special card will also be given, put it in the back cover,

Special card CU, Ryan putting it in the back cover of the book,

You then have to seal the covers tight, and keep the book in the library cafe,

Ryan sealing the book tight; Ryan standing out of the library cafe,

specifically in the shelf just beside the table

Ryan talking with the waiter; slipping the book in
the shelf when no one's around.

from there... the book will reach the right person
eventually

Ryan leaving and Tirth's date entering the cafe; she
pulls out the book; top shot she keeps the book, 2
seconds later camera pulls out to

Tirth rotates the face of the book,

grabs the book and reads its name.

RYAN'S PLACE - LATE LATE EVENING

I am completely frozen, we both are dead silent for a couple of seconds.

I finally speak

TIRTH

(softly)

maybe I am the chosen one

RYAN

you are indeed, it is time you start believing it too, magic happens only after we start believing in magic

TIRTH

(sighs heavily)

I'll take your leave Ryan

I get up and walk towards the door,

RYAN

listen...

I turn back to listen,

RYAN

(c'ntd)

I know you came for the card,

That card has a hidden message, you must not try to
open it now, only after the last chapter, not before it

TIRTH

that means this conversation and meeting was
predicted too... and this answer is not your answer

RYAN

you're a smart man Tirth

TIRTH

Take care Ryan.

I leave,

Ryan watches me leave.

STREET - NIGHT

SELF ATTACHED CAMERA SHOT, SLOW
SHUTTER(UNDERCRANKING)

I am walking crowded streets, platforms et cetera.

There's chaos around me but the voices in my head, overlap each other, voices of Lucifer, Father and Ryan, things that they said to me in the past echo in my ears.

TIRTH'S PLACE - NIGHT

I open my house, enter inside and drink water from
a bottle,

LUCIFER

(v.o)

long time no see my friend I turn to look at him.

He is sitting at his usual place, gives a crooked
smile,

LUCIFER

please feel free to have a seat in your own house

I sit, he starts speaking

LUCIFER

you've been on a roller coaster for the past few
days, haven't you?

TIRTH

It's been crazy, yes

LUCIFER

It was meant to be like that,

one last step still remains, how do you feel about
that

TIRTH

what do I have to do now

LUCIFER

you might be thinking that I'll give you all sorts of
riddles and play games with your mind...

To be honest that sounds so much fun but
unfortunately that is not what chapter 3 demands

TIRTH

then what exactly does chapter 3 demand?

LUCIFER

just read the Bible, the Gospel of John, the
Apocryphon of John and the Gospel of Thomas

TIRTH

wait are you, LUCIFER, telling me to read the Bible

LUCIFER

indeed I am, the very moment you finish reading
these books, waste no time and come in the Church
where you met father

TIRTH

(chuckles)

can you even enter the church ?

LUCIFER

(sighs exhaustedly)

ahhhh... all of that horror movie crap lives rent free
inside your head,

I don't need to come anywhere and I don't need to
leave from anywhere

Remember, I AM EVERYWHERE Lucifer
disappears,

I get moved by his answer, get up, take the Bible
and start reading,

A small montage with uplifting/touching music
shows me

reading the books, some extra shots like in the
balcony observing the world, sitting in nature and
reading the books, time lapses, shots of pages I am
reading etc, last shot will be the shot of me watching
the time on my wristwatch 2:45 AM.

(DISSOLVE TO)

CHURCH - NIGHT

EXT Shot of me watching time in my wrist watch;

TIME - 2:55 AM

I am entering the church in this establishment shot

I go in the church, Lucifer is sitting facing Christ, father is also present

LUCIFER

Father, I think you should go home and take some rest now

Father nods, proceeds towards the gate that I just entered, stops for a second, keeps his hand on my shoulder and pats me, he then leaves.

I go towards Lucifer,

TIRTH

I finished all the books

LUCIFER

of course you did...had you not, you would never
have heard the last straw in your lifetime

Doors close by themselves behind, I get startled and
look behind

LUCIFER

CHAPTER NUMBER 3, you will yourself figure
out the title by the end

tell me what were you taught about me when you
were a child

TIRTH

I remember being taught that Lucifer was absolutely
evil. And most people

imagine you as a dark, evil, Satanic being with
horns

LUCIFER

But you now know that the Bible actually describes me as having originated in Heaven as a powerful angel of light. In Ezekiel, I am described as powerful, beautiful, and wise. But then, according to the Bible, I became corrupt and led a revolution in Heaven against God.

But why? Why did I revolt against God? Before we unravel the mystery of this war in Heaven, let's take a closer look at the connection between Jesus, me

and light, keep in mind this connection to light is critical

Jesus himself claims to be the light of the world twice. Once in John 812, where he directly says, "I am the light of the world." And again, in John Nine five when he says, "when I am in the world, I am the light of the world." And in Revelation 20 216, Jesus identifies himself as the Morningstar. "I, Jesus, am the root and the descendant of David, the bright Morningstar."

TIRTH

Yes, Jesus is self-described as a bringer of light to
the world and the morning star. And as you said
earlier, Lucifer is a Latin name that means Light
bringer, and morning star. And in Isaiah 1412, a
verse that many Bible scholars believe describes
you, identifies you as the morning star as well.

TIRTH & LUCIFER

"How you have fallen from Heaven, morning star,
son of the dawn, you have been cast down to the
earth."

TIRTH

Now it is clear that both Christ and Lucifer are light
bringers and are
identified as the morning star.

LUCIFER

But a closer look at Isaiah 1412 reveals more critical
information. Notice that Lucifer is also identified as
the Son of the dawn, originated in Heaven and was
then cast to Earth. In mainstream Christianity, Jesus
is portrayed as the Son of God, sent from Heaven to
Earth to save humanity, while Lucifer is portrayed
as the Son of the dawn, having fallen to Earth from
Heaven after starting a revolution in Heaven and
attempting to overthrow God. But could these two
stories actually be intertwined?_(soft whisper)

TIRTH

(chuckles)

you and your love for rhetorical questions

(confused)

but what exactly is Jesus trying to save humanity
from?

LUCIFER

To understand the connection, we have to look
deeper at Lucifer's attempt to overthrow God.
According to the Bible, specifically Ezekiel, Lucifer
wanted to become God. When the revolution against

God failed and Lucifer was cast to Earth, something seemingly strange happened.

TIRTH

Lucifer began to tell humanity that they could become God. And this happens in the Garden of Eden. God told Adam he could eat from every tree except the Tree of Knowledge. And the God commanded him, "you may eat freely from every tree of the Garden, but you must not eat from the Tree of Knowledge, for on the day that you eat of it, you will surely die."

Now, it does seem a little strange that God would make knowledge

forbidden. According to mainstream Christianity, Lucifer was in the Garden of Eden and in the form of a serpent, told Eve she could become like God. The serpent said to her,

LUCIFER

"You will not certainly die, for God knows that when you eat from it, your eyes will be opened and you will be like God, knowing good and evil." Now, of course they ate, and did not die.

The Bible views Lucifer as a being who desires to be God and tells humanity that they can be like God.

The question is, has Jesus ever done the same? In the Gospel of John, it says, "we are not stoning you for any good work, said the Jews, but for blasphemy, because you who are a man, declare yourself to be God." Jesus replied, "Is it not written in your law. I have said you are gods."

The Secret Book of John reveals that it was Jesus in the garden that caused Adam and Eve to eat from the forbidden tree of knowledge.

Jesus said, "as for the tree called the knowledge of good and evil, it is the wisdom of the light. They commanded him not to eat from it.

However, I caused them to eat." The connection between Christ and Lucifer here is crystal clear. And you can see why this made a group of people so angry.

But it's about to get even more intense. You might be wondering, why would Jesus cause them to eat from the Tree of Knowledge and go against God's command? That brings us to our next connection. Because like Lucifer, Jesus wants to overthrow God.

Now does that sound crazy or does that sound crazier. Well, get ready, because there's a mountain of evidence

that says just that. According to the Secret Gospel of John, God is not the true God at all. He's a liar, a deceiver. The true God is actually a pure divine mind that exists in and emanates a realm of light called the Pleroma.

And all things, all beings, all creation, including us, are pieces of and part of the divine mind. The God of the Bible, however, is an evil being of chaos and darkness. A false pretender god. You might call him the Shadow of Light. This evil God created a malformed realm of matter and trapped souls of light into bodies in order to enslave humanity.

Now, in the Secret Book of John, Jesus says that he is the one that causes them to eat so that they will wake up from sleep's, death and be filled with the wisdom of the divine light.

According to many of these books banned by the Church, Jesus Christ isn't the son of the evil creator God. He's the son of the true God. Meaning that he's one of the emanations or forms of the true God as you all are. But we forgot our divine nature, and he came here to remind you'll of it.

He's a messenger from the true God, the divine mind, the realm of pure light. You might even call him the Son of Light. And his mission is to help humanity come to self-knowledge that they are divine and escape the evil creator God. Now does that sound familiar.

that is extremely close to the Bible's description of
Lucifer, the morning star and light bringer, the son
of the dawn or son of light that desired to overthrow
the God of the Bible and bring humanity the
message that they could be like God. Could it be
that

Lucifer is actually the good guy here and the Church
just wants to portray anything and anyone that says
you are God as evil so they can maintain their
power.

LUCIFER

I'm happy to see that you're catching my drift. In
another banned gospel, the Gospel of Thomas, Jesus
reveals we come from the realm of living light and
are the true sons of God. Jesus said if they ask you
where are you from? Reply to them we have come
from the place where light is produced from itself.

It came and revealed itself in their image. When you
come to know yourselves, then you will become
known, and you will realize that it is you who are
the sons of the living father.

Even if you want to discount the books banned by
the Church and go strictly by what's in the Bible,
you have to explain why there is such a huge
difference between the Old Testament God and

Jesus Christ of the New Testament. The God of the Bible is a jealous, vindictive, war machine, even in terms of what's described in the Bible. He drowns the entire world in the flood described in the Book of Genesis.

He accepts Jephthah's daughter as a burnt virgin sacrifice, and he has all the male firstborn children and animals of Egypt killed to intimidate the Pharaoh. He is obsessed with death and violence. And remember, all that comes from the Bible itself, not the banned books. But Jesus is the complete opposite. Jesus preaches a message of love and forgiveness.

In fact, he directly contradicts what God said in the Old Testament. Jesus said, "you have heard that it was

said, an eye for an eye and a tooth for a tooth. But I say to you, if anyone slaps you on the right cheek, turn to him the other also." The difference between the God of the Old Testament and Jesus Christ is so drastic, that many early Christians and groups came to the conclusion that the God of the Old Testament was not the true God. Many of them concluded that he was outright evil, like the Marcian, Cainite Christians, and others, like the Valentinians, they believed that he was a lesser God.

There are so many early Christian groups that came to this conclusion that I don't have the time to list them all here. It wasn't until the Church established orthodoxy in Rome and many books were banned, destroyed, and so-called heretics arrested, that this view was all but destroyed, stamped out, eliminated.

TIRTH

(connecting the dots)

Looking at what the Bible says, there is a clear connection between Jesus and Lucifer in the form of light.

The light of the world on one hand and the light bringer on the other. Both are called the Morning Star.

Mainstream Christianity interprets Lucifer as wanting to be God. And Jesus is called God or the Son of God. Lucifer tells humanity they can be like God, and Jesus alludes to this as well.

In the Gospel of John, Lucifer tells this to Eve when he caused her to eat from the Tree of Knowledge. In the banned book, The Secret Book of John, Jesus says that he was the one in the garden that caused Adam and Eve to eat from the tree. Both Christ and Lucifer share the goal of overthrowing the creator God. Christ is revealed to be a Son of Light and Lucifer is the Son of the dawn. In fact, the vast majority of the Gospel of Thomas is Jesus communicating to the reader that they are beings of light and can become God when they look within and realize their divinity.

Looking at all this evidence, what do you believe?

TIRTH

I'll tell you my position. Lucifer and Christ. They're archetypes. They're symbols, but they're the same archetype. In other words, Lucifer and Christ both represent the idea of someone with knowledge of what reality truly is, choosing to share that knowledge with humanity so humanity can become divine.

It's the archetype of the Illuminated liberator someone who has truly achieved a higher consciousness, that has devoted their lives to liberating humanity through wisdom. That is what Lucifer is. That is what Christ is. They are the same archetype. Tell me I've got it right

LUCIFER

that the card will tell, your wait is finally over, go ahead and grab that card and peel the back cover slowly and carefully

I remove the card out of my pocket and start peeling
the back cover,

I peel it; the back side of the card reveals to be the
card of Jesus (Jesus Christ photo)

I am too stunned to react at first, then start laughing

TIRTH

(laughing and speaking; looking at the card the
whole time)

well played Lucifer, well played...

two sides two archetypes, one hero one villain, Jesus
is the protagonist, but the antagonist, LUCIFER
WAS INNOCENT!

A very bright white light and a strong wind appears
in front of me; I squint eyes and look towards it

Lucifer is already gone

It comes from Jesus Christ's conoclast.

TIRTH

where are you Lucifer ? A voice starts coming from
it.

JESUS

(v.o)

He is everywhere and so am I, and here's your last
message.

When the two make peace in this one house, you say
to the mountain move away and it will move away,
when you align your thoughts and feelings in one
singular force, then you will have the power to
move mountains, you will be the sculptor of your
own life.

Thoughts create intentions and feelings provide the
magnetic pull and this is the secret of conscious
manifestation. Remember, "What we think, we
become". How we think will certainly affect our
future, so carefully choose what thoughts would you
allow to linger in your mind.

TIRTH
why did you choose me

The white light remains silent for a couple of
seconds

JESUS

you already know why The white light disappears

I smile softly

\

TIRTH'S ROOM - NIGHT

I am speaking in front of the tripod and phone set up

TIRTH

we live in a society where people are more obsessed
with dead people than living ones, if I say this to
someone on street they would laugh at me, mock
me, throw stones at me or spare me only because
they would think of me as some crazy lunatic who
has lost his mind. All my life I've made people
laugh, I've been the joker, but today if I don't reveal
the truth, I'll end up being the joke in my own eyes.
I sacrifice myself for the truth that every eye must
watch, every ear must hear and every mind must
realize."

LIBRARY - LATE EVENING

(Documentary set up)

MANAV BHATIA

Tirth made me realize one thing, that I have to
worship someone, and that someone is myself, I am
in the universe and the universe is in me

FAIZAL KHAN

(points at people)

you, me, him, her, him we are all parts of the divine
mind, we are the divine mind, we are Gods.

INTERVIEWER

What exactly happened to Tirth after he uploaded
that video

SMARNI, MANAV, FAIZAL

(split screen) I really wish I knew

TIRTH'S ROOM - NIGHT

30 minutes after the last video

I am in the room without the tripod set up

I hold a gun in my hand pointing straight at my head, a little distant, not touched to my forehead

I take a deep breath, close my eyes

MCU/CU OF HAND - PULL THE SAFETY TRIGGER AND SHOOT

LIBRARY - LATE EVENING

MANAV BHATIA

The greatest secrets spoken about by Tirth spread like wildfire all around the world after Tirth went missing and his videos blew up, he was absolutely right when he said we live in a society that is obsessed with dead and missing people than living ones.

INTERVIEWER

when exactly did his last video come out ?

SMARNI RANDIVE

15 days after he went missing, he scheduled it to that day

Also a used gun was found at his place, but his body was never found and that gives me steep hope till date that Tirth is alive

INTERVIEWER

come again...

SMARNI RANDIVE

It gives me steep hope

INTERVIEWER

no the part before that

SMARNI RANDIVE

a used gun was found at his place but his body was
never found

TIRTH'S ROOM - NIGHT

1.   (Tripod setup)

I am speaking in front of the camera,

TIRTH

If u ever come across this story, then your mind was selected by God, you better know which one, to finally be freed... so enjoy the red pill

I get up; turn off my camera and schedule the video's upload,

I sign out of my YouTube account, shut the laptop, grab a gun, point it at my head and take one last deep breath, and close my eyes

I shoot; the bullet comes out of the gun but dissolves mid air,

My third eye opens; I dissolve into the atmosphere and the gun falls down.

Black out for a second,

TIRTH

(v.o)

In the end, god asks for a sacrifice so I decide to
sacrifice myself to let you know, whether you call it
Paatal, Jahanam or hell, whether u call it swaraga,
Jannat or heaven, whether

you call him Asur, Shaitaan or the Devil and
whether you call him Ishwar, Khuda or God, you
look into yourself and you see them lying WITHIN
YOU,

THIS IS YOUR WAKE UP CALL TO REALITY.

& As of me,

अंत ही आरम्भ है

THE END is just A RISE OF A NEW
BEGINNING…

AHAM BRAHMASMI !

MISSING

IF YOU HAVE INFORMATION
PLEASE CONTACT
(Phone Number)

Unlock
your
3rd Eye

Your Brain Is
The Garden Of Eden

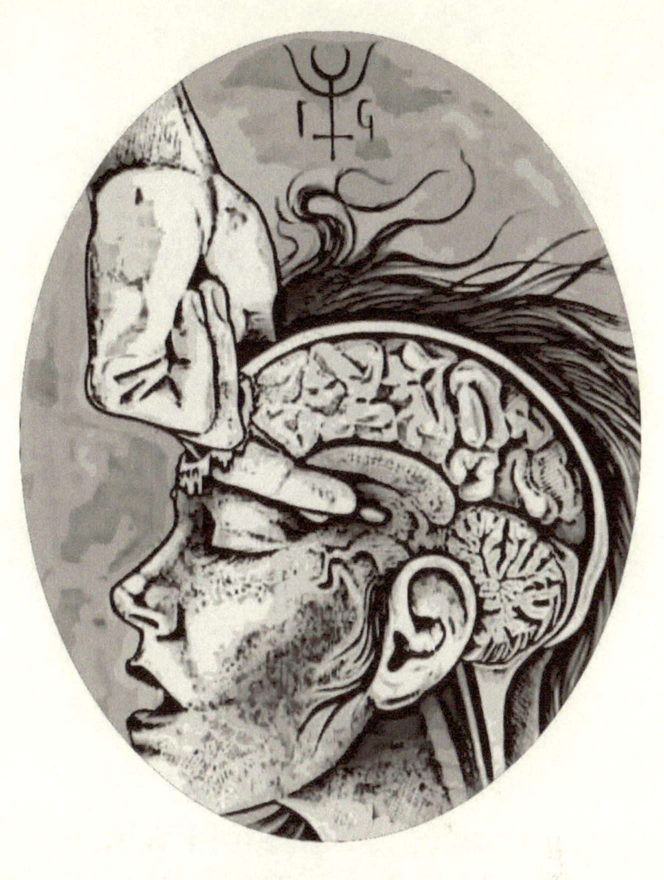

The Pineal Gland Is The Thorne
Of God & The Gateway To
Heaven

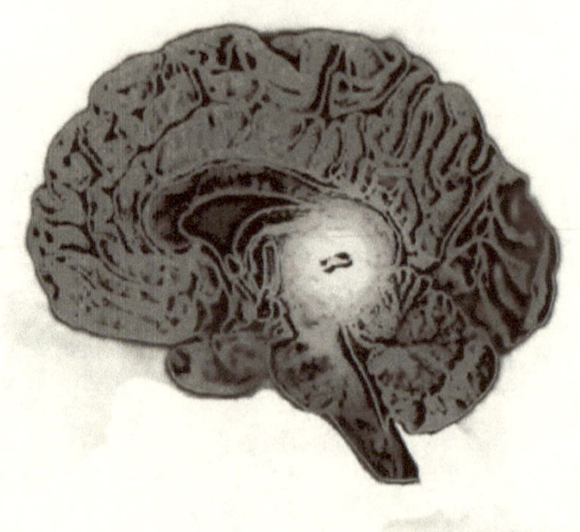

Salvation Is Salt The Brain
Produces A Salt Fluid Which
Goes Down The Spine

You Must Resurrect This Fluid
Through Your Erectional Energy
Back To Your Brain

Which   is   Resh,   A   Hebrew   For   Head.
" Raise Your Salt "

After Raising Your Salt, You Will Have The "key" Into The Kingdom Of Heaven

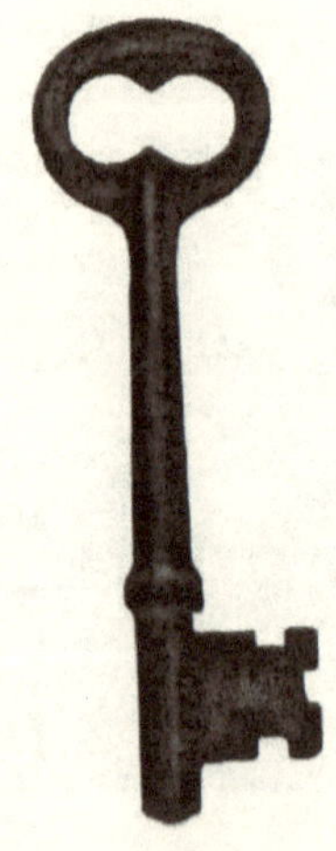

The Realm Beyond The Physical,
To Access The Dimensions Within Your Mind
& Holy Grail

די עליטעס ינוועבטיד רעליגיעז
קאָאפערייישאַנז צו מאַכן איר קוקן
אַרויס זיך ֿפאר מאכט און מאכן איר
זייער שקלאַף

There is No GOD Outside You
YOU ARE GOD